THE RED CHALK

Iris van der Heide

ILLUSTRATED BY
Marije Tolman

Front Street 8 Lemniscaat

ara was bored. The sidewalk was too bumpy to draw on with red chalk. None of her pictures turned out right. She was about to throw her chalk away when she saw Tim on the other side of the street, playing with some marbles. "That looks like fun," Sara thought.

Sara looked in her hand. The red chalk!

"A hopscotch board doesn't have to be perfect,"
Sara thought. She drew a giant one and invited
all of her friends to play.

Then she heard a whistle. Ben was running back. "I forgot to give you this," he said. "Now you can make a new one anytime you want!"

When the rain was gone, Sara returned. "What good is an invisible hopscotch board?" she moaned.

"Sure, I'd like to see that!" Ben said. He
walked away, playing the flute.

Sara threw the hopscotch stone onto the first
square. She was just about to jump when
she felt a drop on her nose—and another
and another. "Rain!" she yelled. She ran off
quickly to seek shelter.

Sara walked until she found Ben, playing hopscotch. "I would love to try that," Sara thought. "Ben, if you blow this whistle, all of the mice in town will follow you wherever you go. Will you trade for your hopscotch board?"

But she couldn't get it right.

"This flute is out of tune!" she said.

Sara blew the flute. A funny noise came out.

She blew it again, hard at first, then softly.

She walked up the hill until she heard some music. Mathilde was blowing a flute. "Wow, that sounds so nice," Sara said. "Look, Mathilde—this is a wishing yo-yo. Every time you roll it up, you can make a wish. Will you trade for your flute?"

"Sure," Mathilde said. "I will wish for a pet rabbit and a new bike!"

Sara ran off with her yo-yo. She rolled it down … but
couldn't get it to go up. She tried again and again.

"This yo-yo is broken," Sara thought with disappointment.

"Rob," Sara said. "Look what I have. If you lick this lollipop, you will become a genius. Will you trade for your yo-yo?"

"Yes!" Rob said, licking the lollipop. "I will invent a spaceship and fly to the moon!"

But she took it out right away. "Yuck, cherry flavor! I don't like cherry."

She ran through the meadow until she saw Rob. A yo-yo danced on his finger. "Wow," Sara thought. "I wish I had one of those."

Sara put the lollipop in her mouth.

"I have something special to show you," Sara said.
"These are real pearls from the ocean." She held out
the marbles. "Will you trade for your lollipop?"

"I'd love to," Sam replied.

She ran off to the beach, where she found Sam. Sam had a bright red lollipop. "Mmm, I really would like that lollipop," Sara thought.

Sara clicked the marbles together.
Then she tried rolling them on the
sidewalk. The marbles went in all
different directions. "What a pity,"
Sara thought. "They're no fun at all."

"Tim," she said. "Look. This is magic chalk. Everything you draw with it will come to life. Do you want to trade for your marbles?"

"Sure!" Tim said. He drew a dragon right away.

For Nina, Jari and Lola
I.H.

For Ramon
M.T.